7/98

Perrywinkle's Magic Match

by Ross Martin Madsen
pictures by Dirk Zimmer

DIAL BOOKS FOR YOUNG READERS
New York

Dial easy-to-read

To Mom and Dad—Lois and Chris—with love
R.M.M.

To James and Sean
D.Z.

Published by Dial Books for Young Readers
A Division of Penguin Books USA Inc.
375 Hudson Street
New York, New York 10014

The Dial Easy-to-Read logo is a registered trademark of
Dial Books for Young Readers,
a division of Penguin Books USA Inc.,
® TM 1,162,718.

First Edition
1 3 5 7 9 10 8 6 4 2

Library of Congress Cataloging in Publication Data
Madsen, Ross Martin.
Perrywinkle's magic match/by Ross Martin Madsen
pictures by Dirk Zimmer.—1st ed.
p.   cm.
Sequel to: Perrywinkle and the book of magic spells.
Summary: Nevermore, the pet crow, comments as
Perrywinkle and Andromeda compete for superiority in magic
until they learn that the best way is to do it together.
ISBN 0-8037-1108-5 (trade).—ISBN 0-8037-1109-3 (lib. bdg.)
[1. Magic—Fiction. 2. Wizards—Fiction.
3. Competition (Psychology)—Fiction. 4. Crows—Fiction.]
I. Zimmer, Dirk, ill. II. Title.
PZ7.M2664Pg 1997 [E]—dc20 95-45185 CIP AC

The full-color artwork was prepared using black ink,
colored pencils, watercolor, and acrylic paint.
Reading Level 2.1

Contents

THE GLOP

"Your dad will be mad!"

squawked Nevermore,

Perrywinkle's pet crow.

"Those are *his* magic books."

"Hush your beak,"

said Perrywinkle.

"You are going to get into trouble,"

warned Nevermore.

"Not a chance," said Perrywinkle.

"I have practiced every day

since I earned my magic wand."

"Me too," said Andromeda,

Perrywinkle's friend.

"Practice does not always

make perfect," said Nevermore.

"It worked for my father,

the Great Wizard!" said Perrywinkle.

"Besides," said Andromeda,

"we want to make something

to show him what we have learned.

Let's make him a pet.

It could keep him company too."

Perrywinkle waved his magic wand.

A book floated down from the shelf.

"PET POTIONS MADE EASY," he read.

"I will say the directions,"

said Andromeda.

"No, I will," said Perrywinkle.

Andromeda was not happy.

"THREE CUPS BURNED WATER.

ONE CROSS CROW'S FEATHER."

"Not another feather,"

groaned Nevermore.

Perrywinkle finished reading,

"TWO GIRL WINKS (BOTH EYES).

BOY SPIT. MIX WELL, SAY SPELL."

"Why does my part always hurt?"

asked Nevermore.

"Magic can be painful,"

said Perrywinkle.

He pulled a tail feather.

"Ouch!" yelled Nevermore.

"Here is the burned water,"

said Andromeda.

Perrywinkle poured it

into the Potion Pot.

Then he added Nevermore's feather.

Andromeda winked once with each eye.

Perrywinkle spat.

He stirred the Potion Pot.

"I will say the spell,"

Andromeda said.

"No, I will," said Perrywinkle.

"Boys do magic better."

Andromeda glared as Perrywinkle said,

"PET APPEAR, FOR MY DAD.

PET APPEAR, YOU WILL BE—"

"MAD!" Andromeda shouted.

"Oh, no," moaned Perrywinkle.

"The last word is *GLAD*."

"Now we are *all* in trouble,"

said Nevermore.

"Fly for your lives."

11

The Potion Pot danced in a circle,

then hopped five feet into the air.

A purple glop splashed on the floor.

The glop grew two arms, ten fingers,

and a mouth with very sharp teeth.

Perrywinkle and Andromeda crawled

onto the sofa.

"ABRA-CA-DABRA!" Perrywinkle said.

The glop changed to orange and green.

"Nice colors," said Nevermore.

"ALI-KA-ZAM," said Andromeda.

The glop grew red eyes.

"Now it can see!" shouted Nevermore.

Perrywinkle and Andromeda climbed

onto the bookshelf.

"Where are the wands?"

asked Andromeda.

"Near the glop monster's mouth,"

Perrywinkle said.

Nevermore flew between glop fingers

and grabbed a wand in his beak.

He dropped it into Perrywinkle's hand.

"GO AWAY, GLOP," Perrywinkle said.

The monster disappeared.

"Close call," Andromeda said.

"It is all your fault,"

said Perrywinkle. "I told you

boy magic is better than girl magic."

"No way!" Andromeda yelled.

And she stomped out the door.

MAGIC SHOW-OFF

The next day Andromeda was still mad.

"What is wrong?" Perrywinkle asked.

"Boy magic is not better than

girl magic," Andromeda answered.

"I can prove it is," said Perrywinkle.

"Don't show off," warned Nevermore.

Perrywinkle waved his wand.

A fence became a dragon,

and a tree became a knight.

"Chase each other," Perrywinkle said.

They came after him instead.

"Run!" Nevermore yelled.

Perrywinkle dropped his wand and ran.

"Help!" Perrywinkle cried.

Andromeda picked up the wand.

"ABEL-CA-BABEL!" she shouted.

The dragon became a fence with wings

and flew away.

The knight became a tree with feet

and ran away.

"Thanks," said Perrywinkle.

"Don't mention it," said Andromeda.

"Aren't you surprised

girl magic saved you?"

"A little," said Perrywinkle,

"but you made a mistake.

My feet are tree roots.

Could you change them?"

"I did," said Andromeda.

She dropped his wand and walked away.

It piled up on the floor around them.

Dinah's and Polly's hair curled

around desks and chairs.

Hair was everywhere.

"Stop it!" Andromeda shouted.

Perrywinkle spelled

"H-A-I-R G-O A-W-A-Y."

It did. Everyone was bald.

"Hair today, gone tomorrow,"

said Nevermore.

Andromeda waved her wand.

Everybody's hair grew back.

Ms. Applebest sent

Perrywinkle and Andromeda home

with notes for their parents.

On the way Perrywinkle said,

"Thanks for helping,

but boy magic is still better."

"Oh, really?" said Andromeda.

And Perrywinkle tripped over the tail

she gave him.

MIXING MAGIC

"Is not better!" said Andromeda.

"Is so better!" said Perrywinkle.

They stood nose to nose.

Sparks came out of their wands.

"You have gone too far,"

said Nevermore.

"What is wrong?"

asked the Great Wizard.

"Perrywinkle says boy magic is better

than girl magic," Andromeda said.

"It *is* better!" said Perrywinkle.

"We tried to make a pet for you,

but Andromeda made a monster."

The Great Wizard smiled.

"You can do magic alone," he said,

"but when you practice with a friend,

you have to learn to work together.

Two people's magic

is always better than one."

"Exactly!" said Nevermore.

"I'm sorry," Perrywinkle said.

"Anyone can make a mistake,"

Andromeda said.

"Why don't you try that spell again?"

said the Great Wizard.

"See what you two friends can do."

"Great," grumbled Nevermore.

"There goes another feather."

Andromeda poured the water

into the pot. She winked.

Perrywinkle spat and stirred.

They said the spell together.

"Look out!" squawked Nevermore.

"It is another glop!"

But Perrywinkle held the pot,

and Andromeda pulled out

a fair-feather-friend.

"Now," Perrywinkle told Nevermore,
"when we need a feather for a spell,
it won't always be painful for you."

The fair-feather-friend stared

at Nevermore.

"My feathers are better

than your feathers," she said.

"Oh, no," wailed Nevermore.

"Here we go again."